REVENGE
Of The
ANGELS

Ted Peters

Copyright © 2014 by Ted Peters

Revenge Of The Angels
by Ted Peters

Printed in the United States of America

ISBN 9781498401319

All rights reserved solely by the author. The author guarantees all contents are original and do not infringe upon the legal rights of any other person or work. No part of this book may be reproduced in any form without the permission of the author. The views expressed in this book are not necessarily those of the publisher.

Scripture.quotations taken from the New American Standard Bible-Catholic Version. Copyright © 1969 by The Thomas Nelson Publishers. Used by permission. All rights reserved.

This book is a work of fiction. Names, characters, places and incidents are products of the author's imagination or used fictitiously. Any resemblance to actual events, locales or persons, living or dead, is completely coincidental.

www.xulonpress.com

INTRODUCTION

In the next two years more people will die in the world by abortion than died in seven major American wars. In the Revolutionary War 25,000 people died, a majority from diseases. In the War of 1812 there were 15,000 casualties. During the Mexican-American War just over 13,000 people perished. In the Civil War the U.S lost 625,000. During World War I, 10 million military and 7 million civilians died. World War II cost the lives of 60 million or more souls. Estimates of deaths during the Vietnam War range from 1 to 3 million. Sadly, the conflict casualty tally for the last 200 years is nearly 80 million.

In the United States there are more than 1.2 million abortions every year with less than 1% linked to rape or incest. Since the landmark legal decision of Roe v. Wade in 1973, 57 million lives have been terminated in America by abortion. Around the world there are more than 40 million abortions performed every year! Since international figures have been kept there have been more than 1.3 billion abortions.

Going forward the data will be more difficult to track. In many countries 20 to 30% of all abortions are now performed with medications dispensed by doctors, not in surgical clinics. Privacy concerns will likely trump the desire for accurate records. It is estimated that 1 to 5% of all women terminate a pregnancy annually. There are 70,000 maternal deaths and 8 million medical complications a year from abortion.

The practice is widespread and accepted. It is seen as a quick way to end an inconvenient accident. It is legally protected in many countries and even encouraged by overcrowded nations. In truth, it is relatively safe, cheap and available. But, truth be told, it *is* murder. A fertilized ovum quickly develops a beating heart. Great philosophers and religious leaders throughout history have proscribed killing. But now you can kill as long as you do it when the courts say you can. Over the decades, religious groups have kept up their protests matched loudly by "pro-choicers." Big providers make fortunes by the practice. So who is right? What does God want? What can be done to stop the killing? The God of the Old Testament punished the whole world with the Great Flood and select populations during the Passover and in Sodom and Gomorrah. How might God go about ending abortion? What would it look like?

For my deceased parents, my very alive and loving family and the religious and lay teachers who have helped me grow….. T.P.

Chapter 1

The young priest was excited but nervous. He had arrived at the run-down St. Michael's monastery in the dark and found it cold and frightening. He was to join fellow standout students who had been sent to Rome for higher studies. They were tops in their classes in seminaries around the world. These few were possibly chosen to become the thinkers, the planners, the new blood who could invigorate the Church.

Still more frightening, today he would meet the brilliant teachers sent to this monastery from Catholic nations around the world. What mysteries would he learn? What was so important that these new graduates, ready to go out to a life of service in churches that desperately needed them, were pulled away for a summer? Why did the Church do this? How much would he have to study? How tough would this be?

Matthew Edwards came from a well-to-do family. Not rich, but the children had what they needed. He never struggled. He had no desire for money or the will to work hard to get it. He was brought up as a religious young man. To his parents religion gave meaning to life. They believed all good things came from God. From fifth grade through high school he was an altar boy leader. He went to church every Sunday and several afternoons or evenings during the week. He was also a Boy Scout. He took music lessons on various instruments. Despite all these activities, he was first in his class from elementary to high school. His guidance counselors knew Matthew could go to any college he desired. They expected medicine, engineering or law. His choice of a seminary college surprised everyone but his local priest.

He was tall, blonde and handsome but never had any meaningful relationships with women. He enjoyed going to church and decided he could live a good life and best serve God as a priest. He was devoted to his five younger siblings. He donated a kidney to a brother born with an inherited disorder and spent his last summer-long vacation recovering from surgery. He did well in the seminary and was considered among the best students his professors could remember. They had groomed him to become a scholar or administrator but Matthew wanted to be a regular parish priest.

Matthew wanted to serve in a church near his hometown. The city had grown since 9/11 when thousands of families left New York for safer locations. Many still commuted to work but spent weekends at their new homes and these filled the churches. The old priests in the Northeast were tired and looked forward to having new blood to assist with weekend services. Now one of the best candidates had been taken away for "special studies" in Rome.

When Matthew awoke in his small room he found a note that had been slipped under the door: "Report to room 200 at 9 a.m." Oatmeal, toast and coffee were on a tray in the hall. The food was satisfactory but not as good at his mother's cooking. He assumed he would be going to an auditorium to meet his fellow chosen ones, perhaps to watch a video or listen to a rousing speech. He saw no one in the hallways. Room 200 was a small study next to the library. There were shelves with hundreds of books, comfortable chairs and fairly good lighting. He began to snoop.

Monsignor John G. Borgogno was a tall, distinguished, gray-haired Italian-American. He looked a bit stern. He walked into the study and dropped some books on the table.

"Matthew Edwards, how was your breakfast?"

"Fine, sir."

"Not like your mother Mary's cooking, right?"

"No, Monsignor, but good enough to get the day started. How do you know my mother's name, sir?"

"Each of us has been given a portfolio to study on the lives of our new students. There is only a small group here this year and you were assigned to me. I think we'll work well together in this special task Rome has given us. We are here for focused prayer. Do you know what that means?"

"Not exactly, sir."

"Well, it means we will be selecting a specific issue or problem facing the Church in the world, focusing on that and praying to remedy it. We will talk about the issue and how it affects everyone. Then we will pray. Maybe we can help solve the problem. Monks have a long tradition of group prayer and that's why this monastery was chosen for us to gather. I am your guide and you are to be my inspiration."

The Monsignor went on: "I've brought some books for you to look at. They're some of my favorites on the Church and the power of prayer. I want you to spend the day looking them over. Read what you like now and meditate tomorrow. You'll meet your fellow students at exercise before supper. Everyone starts with different goals and ideas at this school. Enjoy them as friends, but you may not understand each other. I still don't know why they dropped mandatory Latin! Tonight I want you to begin to think about the problem you and I should work on. I'll see you Wednesday at 9."

The handsome man in the black suit and white collar stood up, smiled and walked out of the room. The heavy door closed with a thud. Matthew poured a glass of water from the pitcher on the table. On the tray was a handwritten note that read, "Gymnasium at 4, supper at 6." He began to read through the books on the table but became bored. The library shelves were filled with dusty old volumes. In a bound metal box he found a leather file listing members of the monastery staff. It was marked "OCCULTUS." Under the heading for "*B*" he found Borgogno. Now this would be an interesting read.

It seems Father John G. Borgogno, now a Monsignor, had been educated in Rome then assigned to various parishes across America. He stayed no more than one or two years at any church then was transferred several states away. Matthew worried there might be a sad, abusive storyline here. All his parishes were listed from east to west but no hometown. No mention of living relatives. Matthew checked his cell phone but it had no bars. He went to the courtyard and was happy to find he had internet access. He searched for newspaper articles from many of Borgogno's former residences. He found testimonials from local papers that praised the priest for his work with the poor, hungry and the critically ill in local hospitals. People he reached out to generally turned the corner. Some of the poor he visited found jobs. A few became lottery winners. Many of his sacraments of Last Rites were thought to be wasted since the ill parishioners often went home before long.

Crowds had attended Father John's masses but few went if he was off or out of town. This did not sit well with his fellow priests. No suggestion of anything improper but transfers came regularly. They didn't openly criticize him but no one wanted him in his parish. Church was about prayer and penance and money in the baskets. This man might be dangerous. Borgogno knew his days as a parish priest were numbered. After being moved from New York to California the Cardinal of Los Angeles made a call to the Vatican.

John Borgogno was made a Monsignor and sent to the Institute for Focused Prayer in Rome. And he was now Matthew's mentor. Wow!

No lunch was provided and at 3:30 Matthew went to his room, put on gym clothes and jogged to the basketball court. There were eleven others gathered for some exercise and stress relief. They all needed it. They looked lost and confused. Not a distinguished-looking group of young graduate priests. They all knew some English, Spanish and French. But everyone knew they had been sent to Rome for a special purpose. Each young priest was assigned to an older, distinguished mentor from their home country. In their initial meetings all the novices had been excited by the prospect of setting out to cure some unspecified worldly evil.

Now they would unwind with some basketball. They all agreed tomorrow they would try to find a soccer ball for some European football. Supper was bland but filling. Very little conversation, and lights were out soon after evening prayers in the chapel. Matthew had been charged with dreaming up a plan to solve a major world problem and tonight he couldn't sleep.

Monsignor Borgogno and young Father Edwards met after two days of meditation.

"What have you come up with Matthew?"

"Well, sir, this is tough. I thought that I love my family and all our friends and neighbors, but mostly I love children. It worried me for many years that young babies who died prematurely and never got baptized couldn't go to heaven. Their souls were in some state of suspended existence between heaven and purgatory. I thanked God when our recent Pope wrote that he did not consider this to be proper teaching. All babies who died without baptism but whose parents had wanted them baptized could go to heaven. I hope it's true. So I am most concerned about those unfortunate souls who never get that chance. Of course, I'm talking about abortion, the scourge of modern civilization. As I have read, every two years there are more lives taken than in all the great wars of the last two centuries. There are over one million abortions every year in America and less than one percent are due to rape or incest. And world-wide there are more than forty million a year! It's disgusting and it has to stop. I can't think of anything more troubling that we as a Church need to challenge. But how? We are not powerful. We don't have the political strength of the "pro-choicers" and the governments that back them. Of course, I hate war and hunger and communism but I'd have to say I would spend my life praying to stop abortion first and foremost."

"Abortion, huh? I see you have been reading and praying Matthew. I have very strong feelings on the subject myself but many in my generation have given up hope of ever changing the situation. My initial impression is that I can't think of anything more wicked or demonic than the mass slaughter of innocents that occurs every year with official blessing. Government leaders turn their backs on this injustice. They sanctify it with court rulings. And they force people to subsidize murder with their taxes. It is truly unbelievable. Yes, it is a worthy project for us to work on. Now I think we should retreat to study and pray some more. Let us draft a prayer. Tell me tomorrow what you propose."

In the morning Matthew ate his breakfast and hurried to room 200. Monsignor Borgogno was there with some dusty Old Testament books.

"Matthew, where do we start?"

"Well, Monsignor, I was thinking.... we always learned that everyone has a guardian Angel to watch over him. But I don't know about the unborn. Do they have one? And you know, in the New Testament God got pretty mild and peaceful. He sent His only Son to teach us about love and kindness.....warm and fuzzy stuff. We need some Old Testament fire and brimstone, maybe an Angel of Death! But perhaps God has gotten too mellow for that kind of action. You think we can pray to anyone in particular to help us with our mission?"

"Well, I have always believed there were Angels looking out for us. They're all around us. We just can't see them. Maybe they only appear to very special people, holy people.... like Gabriel to Mary or the Angel who spoke to the Apostles at the tomb on the Resurrection. I've studied some old Hebrew texts. The Jews brought back scrolls from Babylonian captivity with names of the Archangels. They taught about Gabriel, herald to the prophets. And Raphael, the healer. Of course, Lucifer was the fallen Archangel who rebelled against God and was violently driven out of heaven and cast into hell by the Archangel Michael. Michael, spear in hand, protector of God's domain, foe of God's enemies. I also know of Archangel Metatron, the highest of the Angels. He is the powerful scribe and overseer of all the Angels, described in brilliant white light. Maybe we could focus our prayers on him, Matthew. Maybe he would dispatch Michael and have him come to the earth and do whatever it takes to stop the slaughter of the innocents. What do you think?"

"Well, nobody prays to Angels anymore. I don't know if you can. I mean, I don't know if you're allowed to. Maybe they only respond to God's orders. They were sent by Him to carry messages."

"Maybe we can, son, maybe we can. Perhaps God is sick of the decadence in the world and would turn his head and let an Angel come down to bring justice to the earth. It would take powerful prayer but I can't think of a more worthy cause. And that's why we're here this summer. I believe we can accomplish great things."

Matthew grew excited. His eyes lit up. "This is a wonderful challenge but a bit frightening. What if we got what we were asking for? How would we know if an Archangel came here? What if there were death and destruction, would that be our fault?"

"Matthew, if a few well-placed deaths somehow stopped forty million abortions a year.... if that were possible....don't you think that would be worth it?"

"I don't think I would want to be responsible for any deaths."

"Well, maybe you're not up to this task. But I think it's exciting. I've spoken to a few of the other proctors in the monastery this week.

Many are known for charitable works or setting up schools. They're devout and dedicated men but they haven't come up with much here yet: "stamp out war; heal the sick; stop famine." Even Jesus said we'll always have the poor and starving. Help thy neighbor, yes. But we're talking about the elimination of genocide bigger than the Nazi atrocities. Aren't you interested in helping, Matthew?"

"Well, yes I am, I guess. It's a bit strange though. I have to be honest, sir, I've read about you. I found the Institute staff folder and you're in it. Pretty impressive travels."

"I've served in a lot of parishes, yes. And I hope you don't have any mistaken ideas about my transfers."

"No, Monsignor, not at all. In fact, I did some internet browsing of American papers and they were all quite impressive. It seems you brought peace and happiness to many of your parishioners. If I may say so, I'm not sure where your fire and brimstone comes from."

"I'm not sure, Matthew, but now it's inside me and clawing to get out. I believe I need you and the others in this conclave to focus and pray with me. Are you in?"

"I'm in!"

Excited about this summer project and his new partner, the Monsignor reported after dinner to the chief of the monastery, Senior Bishop Ignatius Francisco. "Your Excellency, I have great hopes for my project this summer. My young charge is bright and energetic and the others are up to the task as well. Together we will strive to stamp out what I believe is the greatest evil on earth.....abortion."

"You propose to do that through meditation.... here?"

"Yes, Bishop, we plan to try with a summer of intense prayer."

"Humm, I guess OK. Good luck and keep me updated on this fantasy of yours. You know, we will always have wars and murders. They kind of give the whole Church a focus for weekly services....a way to get people in on a Sunday. I'm not sure what would happen if all our big problems were magically solved! And I don't know if you could make this happen by the prayers of your little group."

Francisco was a PR man. He arranged international trips and seminars...a religious "travel agent." He was also to keep tabs on American clerics, make them happy and keep them in line. Most of all, he was to secure funding streams from the United States to Rome. An international conclave to attack abortion was way beyond his expertise. After the Monsignor left his office, Francisco pondered the development. This man, Borgogno, had a reputation that preceeded him. He was a doer, a pious go-getter. And now he had come to dominate this conlave. Just what if something weird happened? The old vicar picked up his phone. He dialed from memory the back line to the OPF, the Office for the Preservation of the Faithful. "Yes?"

"Your Eminence, there may be a problem."

The next day, after morning mass, Borgogno proposed his plan to the group. He felt he had the approval of the Bishop for them to spend their summer praying for the elimination of abortion. This would be in keeping with the new Pope's stated mission of helping the downtrodden. He asked Matthew to read aloud the prayer they had developed and invited the other study pairs to feel free to propose more. They would meet twice a day for formal prayers. The small band of dedicated young men and respected senior clerics from around the world were hungry for a religious problem to solve. Throughout history monks had gathered at this location to pray secretly. You could almost feel their presence and hear their chants. The subjects of their efforts were never made known. The delegates today were eager to take on a new challenge.

Matthew recited the prayer he and the Monsignor had developed: "Dear God, almighty Father, creator of the universe, hear us. Listen to your servants as we pray to you. Lord, your people need your intervention. We beseech you to stop the slaughter of the innocents. We deplore the loss of millions of souls that long to be with you in heaven. Your faithful children have prayed for decades to overturn the injustice of this immoral act but have been unsuccessful. We turn to you now to stop the genocide. Let loose your Angels. Send them down from heaven to fight this atrocity with your righteous vengeance. Archangel Metatron, scribe and overseer of the Angels, the children of God ask you to send us Michael, the conqueror of Lucifer. The satanic forces at work in our land can only be overcome by the same God-given power used to drive Satan into hell. Michael, warrior, protector of heaven, come to us and save the souls of the unborn. Thousands of years ago God sent floods, pestilence, and the Angel of Death to the firstborn of the Egyptians to save His people and establish His dominion on the earth. Do as you must to redeem these slaughtered souls for the Father, the Son and the Holy Spirit. We ask this in God's holy name. Amen."

For the remainder of the summer the twelve pairs met daily to send their voices to heaven. More passages were added in various languages. The prayers were easily learned by the groups from the four corners of the earth. Day and night they also recited litanies, novenas and chants, many taken from the monastery's library. The old proctors had a feeling something good was happening. They felt excited every morning and at peace every night. Francisco never joined them but spoke occasionally with Borgogno. The elders were told the Bishop had important meetings at the Vatican. And so he did.

Chapter 2

Southport, Texas was an up-and-coming metropolis. Big business, big sports and oil tycoons….a junior Dallas. They loved their fast cars and fast girls. And starting in high school they idolized their sports stars. The high school football team was one of the best in the state. Every Friday night large crowds turned out to watch the team crush their opponents. There were post-game dances in the gym but most of the stars didn't go. They were at private parties funded by rich school boosters. There was always plenty of booze "accidentally" left behind the bar in the mansion basements.

Things were tense at the school this week. Friday was the district playoff game. If they won, they were going to states. If they lost, there would be hell to pay. James Mack was the star senior quarterback. This was his second year as the starter and he quickly became a local hero. He had money, a fast car and good looks. He was assured of a football scholarship, a free ride to the college of his dreams. He dumped his junior year girlfriend, a pretty brunette, because of some disagreements. He had tried this semester to date the cutest blonde at the school, Holly Jones.

Holly was a pretty and smart senior. Despite her good looks she did not casually date around. She was serious about her plans to be an accountant and someday join her father's firm. She wanted to go to the University of Texas for a special accounting/MBA program.

After many pleas from Jimmy Mack, Holly had still refused to go out on even the safest of dates. Jimmy hoped this week would be different. He would tell her he didn't think he could win the big game without her being there. And if they did win, he wanted to take her out for a burger after the game and maybe stop at a friend's party. For some reason, this time she said yes. Maybe she wanted a little fling before college. She would meet him in the school lobby after the game, win or lose.

Of course, Southport won and moved on to the state finals. Jimmy set a record for touchdown passes and he felt confident they would win the championship the following Saturday. Tonight he wanted to celebrate and Holly was there waiting for him in the lobby. He texted his mother: "Probably won't be home tonight. Will crash at Tim's house after his party. Will be too tired to drive. Best to be safe. Tell dad. Love....Me."

Holly texted home: "Might stay with Judy tonight. Everybody is psyched about winning the game so we'll all party a bit. I will be safe. See you in the morning." She knew Judy would cover her if needed.

Joined by another couple for burgers, Jimmy was very polite. That was always the case until he started drinking. After dinner, they drove in his cool convertible Mustang to Tim Patton's party. Tim had a huge house with a great basement. There was a pool table, darts and a big air hockey game. Jimmy excelled at all three. There was a huge TV with surround sound. One of the players brought a video of the game made in the TV booth that night. It was great to watch, especially with ice cold beer. Conveniently, Tim's parents were on a business trip so they had the place to themselves this weekend. Jimmy asked Holly if she was covered for the night or did he have to take her home? "No problem." He was home free.

After a few more drinks Jimmy took Holly upstairs. Enough beer, he thought. She might pass out soon or get sick. He found a bedroom, locked the door and fell onto the bed with her. "I want you."

"No Jimmy, you're a great guy but let's get to know each other better first."

"We know each other fine."

"Jimmy, this is not a good time for me. We can't. It's not safe."

"Don't worry, I'll be careful. Give me a present for winning the game." His heavy body pinned Holly to the bed as he pulled off her jeans. She was too tired to fight.

When Jimmy awoke from his stupor the next morning, there was a note on his jeans: "Got a ride home from Judy. I'm scared. This was stupid." The following weekend, Southport narrowly lost in the state finals. It was a disappointment to the team and the whole town but

Jimmy knew how to lift his spirits. He would call Holly for a date. That would make him feel better. Holly had to leave town for a relative's wedding so the date was off. She would see him the following week.

The two met at the coffee shop after school one day. When he walked in he could tell she had been crying. "I missed my period. I'm never late. God, I'm scared."

"What the hell are you talking about? Aren't you on the pill or something?"

"No I'm not. I tried it once but it made me sick. And I haven't dated anybody this year anyway. I really wanted to go out with you but it all happened too fast. I wasn't ready, Jimmy. Now what?"

"Go to a doctor or a clinic or something. I'll pay for the visit."

"I'll go to the school nurse first and see what she thinks."

"Don't you mention my name, dammit."

The drugstore test recommended by the nurse was positive. Holly didn't know what to do. She knew if she talked to her mother, she would tell her father and he would kill her or have a nervous breakdown or something. Holly was the oldest. She was the smartest. She was supposed to set a good example for her younger brother and twin sisters, go to college and be a professional. Again she planned to meet Jimmy.

Jimmy was hoping the worst would not happen but he was a man and could handle it. He was tough and smart and had money. Besides, he had been down this road before. The two met at the coffee shop again. She told him the bad news and cried. This would so disappoint her parents. Jimmy told her not to worry. Her parents would never know. He would take care of it. They would go to a special clinic he knew about. He would go with her and pay for it.

"Are you talking about an abortion? I don't know if I can do that."

"Well you better start thinking straight and convince yourself fast you *are* going to do that! You're not going to screw up your life and mine by letting this go on. I'm going to be a college quarterback and maybe even turn pro. You're not going to ruin that. I'll call tomorrow to make an appointment. That's that. Get over it."

The women's clinic near Houston was a big, sterile gray building with a sign reading "Health and Wellness Center." Holly thought this was rather odd considering the doctor there probably killed off more people every year than populate a lot of small towns in Texas. She filled in a new patient form and waited to go back. She told the secretary she was just there for information and to talk to somebody about her options. The lady said "Options? Girl, most people know what they want by the time they get here. You want to talk options, talk to your momma or friends. We're very crowded and time here is limited. You get a few minutes with the doctor and you better make your mind up fast. Did you bring money?" Jimmy said he had money and he was sure Holly would be fine.

As they were led down a long hallway to an exam room, Holly heard a motor noise and muffled cries. Through an open door to an empty room she saw a glass container in a pump filled with bloody material. She felt like puking. She knew she couldn't do this but she was so afraid of her parents' reactions and of ruining her future.

The handsome, well-dressed Doctor Bill Sherwood came in with his nurse. He looked at the young couple and knew they were upset. Was he really concerned about her or was he nervous about losing a potential customer? "Listen, don't be nervous. This is no big deal. I do dozens of these every day. We give you some medicine. You won't feel much. It's in and out. I just have to check you first. When was your last period?"

"I'm not really sure, sir. Not long ago."

"Oh!"

After his exam the doctor looked at the nurse and said "I think we need an ultrasound in here. Holly, this is going to cost you a little bit extra but we really need a picture here."

"I don't want to hear a heartbeat or any of that stuff, Doc."

"Yes, I know." After a few minutes the doctor looked at the nurse and the young couple and said "It's twins....But we can still do this. You have to decide fast." Holly began sobbing. She wanted to leave. God, she wanted to talk to her mother and friends and her aunt. She needed help. What if her mother had had an abortion? She wouldn't even know her little twin sisters.

"I don't know."

But Jimmy said, "No way lady. This was your fault for not protecting yourself and you're not going to screw up everything now. Do it. Get it over with. Go ahead Doc, I have the money." The doctor recognized Jimmy. Of course, he was the Southport quarterback. But he also remembered the boy from his junior year when he came to the clinic with a pretty brunette girl who had a similar "problem." But that was kept between the guys. Holly scribbled her signature on a piece of paper and was given some medication. In an hour she was getting into the Mustang no longer a mother-to-be.

At the end of the day the doctor sat down to count his proceeds for the week... tens of thousands. What production! Very busy. And he was doing what so many people wanted. How could anybody fault him? He was good at it–quick, clean and confidential. The few protesters who came around were dealt with by the police. He had actually seen demonstrators in the front yard who had brought their daughters to him over the years to take care of their "problems!" For sure, he couldn't mention that. But how ironic and phony. He gave all the clinic workers a crisp hundred dollar bill for their weekly bonus and went to the country club for a quick round of golf. It was a beautiful day to drop the top on the Porsche.

Jimmy drove Holly home. She was too sick to stop for dinner and too messed up to think about partying that night. Jimmy called his friends to go drinking. Over beer with his buddies he decided not to call Holly any more. She was trouble. He'd wait to find a hotter babe in college who took precautions. Problem solved.

Suffering extreme regret and depression, Holly soon began to reconsider her plans for a double degree at the university. She told her mother she was confused and perhaps would take a year off and get a job to pay for some therapy sessions.

Chapter 3

The summer program at the monastery ran into fall. When it wrapped up all the participants were excited. They hoped for some response to their prayers. The sky was brighter and the days were hotter than most autumns. The proctors ended the conclave by thanking the graduates for participating and livening up the old place. Surely God would reward them in some way but perhaps not quickly. They all went to pack for flights later that day to start work in parishes. Most were assigned to small out-of-the-way churches far from any cathedrals. The Monsignor would teach freshman bible study in an obscure south Florida seminary.

Borgogno met later with the Bishop. He thought some of the young priests might be asked to stay on to meet the Pope as a reward. Maybe they could continue the seminar's work in some way. Francisco said it was not his decision and his superior, the Cardinal in charge of the OPF, did not really see the continuance of the conclave as a necessary activity. There was no money for the group and His Eminence had decided the monastery would be torn down to make room for a new Catholic school for orphans. Who could oppose that? Borgogno thought perhaps he had wasted his summer.

In postwar Germany many businesses had begun to thrive as commercial shipping became safe again. Most U-boats were sunk or destroyed in port. After the horrors of the Holocaust, minds turned to money. And a growing business was medical device manufacturing. In Berlin, a wealthy family with medical and engineering experience invested in factories that made vacuum equipment. These pumps were used in commercial buildings and in flood rescue efforts. They were also used in operating rooms around the world to clear blood from body cavities in major surgery. But in another department, a decorated war veteran began developing a different side of the family business. The 'Sogink' division provided a vacuum model designed specifically for pregnancy termination. Nobody made a better one. Hospitals and clinics around the world quickly began purchasing these pumps which lasted for a few years of heavy use. The manufacturing plant expanded and storage facilities for replacement parts were built in Dresden and Hamburg. Tubing, rubber gaskets and netting were sold by the thousands monthly. Like companies trying to copy the Swiss watch, competitors of the Sogink pump did not last long. The Texas Health and Wellness Center and most other clinics in the United States used the German Sogink. Busy offices had four or five going at all times. Without these pumps it would be lights out for the big abortion centers. The Sogink owners knew it and their factories were heavily guarded. The business thrived over the decades.

The Berlin facility was a large stone structure built on the grounds of an old castle on the Spree River. It was solid and imposing. The gate to the bridge over the Spree was guarded and anyone entering needed a photo ID. There were dormitories for those who lived far away offering cheap boarding and a cafeteria. Two shifts ran sixteen hours a day. The night crew focused on maintenance and repair of machinery. Twelve pairs of workers made constant night rounds with only a few coffee breaks. Everyone knew what went on there but most didn't care. They just wanted to make a living. Besides, most of these pumps went to the big countries that had defeated and humiliated the German people twice. Good for them....their babies would die while Germany prospered.

Several night workers hated what they did and planned to look for other jobs. It made the older men and women sick to think about the pumps. They never discussed it with their kin. They had planned a Friday/Saturday off to jointly interview for maintenance positions at a new auto plant that was adding a late shift. Auto work would be constructive not murderous. They would not be in Berlin that Saturday.

> The Overseer Metatron said to Michael: "The Lord wishes the wind and fire of his vengeance to cleanse the earth of the demons who steal his souls. Ready your sword. His will be done."

Most of the young priests and their mentors were gathered in Rome's da Vinci Airport waiting for night flights to their homes. They hugged and cried. Would they ever meet again? Would their efforts prove fruitful? Could anyone step forward to limit abortion? They met in a small dining room in the central terminal's restaurant. One last time they prayed, hands joined around the table: "Dear God, almighty Father, creator of the universe, hear us......Michael, warrior, protector of heaven, come to us and save the souls of the unborn.......We ask this in God's holy name, Amen."

Crowds at Berlin's Tegel Airport stared out the terminal windows at a distant yellow-white light in the north. As it grew, the evening sky brightened to daylight and the room became very hot. People started to sweat and removed their fall overcoats. Parents took young children to the shelter of lavatories as they recalled the meteorite that had recently struck a Russian city leveling trees and buildings. The ball of light came faster and faster, grew bigger and brighter and smashed into the ground miles from the airport. Most of the windows in the terminal were smashed inward. The air had an acrid smell. Many of the smaller jets waiting on the tarmac were turned on their sides. The Sogink factory was ablaze.

The airport alarms blared. Fire trucks left their garages and deployed to the terminals as a precaution. Some began hosing down fuel tankers to prevent explosions. Ten city crews made their way to the factory site to douse the flames and determine what could be salvaged. The heat at the site was so intense that the local fire captain kept the trucks far back to prevent autoignition. The trucks quickly exhausted their water supply just to hose down the fields surrounding the old castle. Thick gray smoke lay over the site. No one could see the tall stone walls yet. The captain had his men drag large hoses off the trucks and run them down to the river. The vacuum pumps on the trucks, made by this very company, would draw water into one side and force it out the other onto the smoldering buildings.

The state fire marshall arrived as the river water shot from the ten tankers. The captain told him of the little progress they had made due to the intense heat. Then they began to see through the haze. The fire had burned quickly and intensely. The astounded civil servants stared at each other. There was *nothing* left of Sogink! No wood. No metal frame. No stones or bricks. The buildings had been vaporized. Even up to 1000°F there should be cinders or charcoal residue but there was nothing.....just a field of dirt. What's more, none of the workers could be found. No clothes or body parts. Outside the plant, the only visible damages were broken windows for miles around all of which seemed to have imploded.

The next day church bells rang throughout the country. Flags flew at half-mast. There were no bodies to bury. The Chancellor vowed to rebuild the plant which was so important to the nation's economy and so vital to the health of women around the world. Construction on a bigger and better factory would begin immediately. An emergency fund would be provided to open a few temporary lines for assembling Sogink pumps from the spare parts stored at the Dresden and Hamburg warehouses. The government would match private and insurance funds to provide hundreds of jobs for the unemployed laborers in those cities.

Around Germany, the radio and television broadcasts deplored the loss of the industrious Berliners who had made a name for their town in the post-Cold War international economy. The wall came down and German businesses had thrived. Today many suspected industrial sabotage. In the U.S., talk show hosts raised the possibility of a new form of religious terrorism.... not Islamic, but American fundamentalist. No one could overturn Roe v. Wade. The courts had ruled. Liberal administrations had promoted the right to an abortion for decades and now mandated that taxpayers pay for them via national insurance plans. So it was only logical to consider a right-wing plot. Perhaps they would not burn down the Supreme Court but might have no qualms about an attack on foreign soil....and maybe on American clinics. In Washington, the President ordered all state governors to deploy the National Guard to protect busy abortion clinics. It was not clear he had the authority to do so. The twenty Democratic governors complied. The thirty Republicans ordered extra emergency funds be directed to big city fire departments.

Conservative pundits denied the ability of the religious right to carry out such carnage in the name of God, even to save millions of unborn souls. Besides, the technical expertise needed for such an enormous attack would have to involve high-level military officials willing to defect from civilian control and deliver some new weapon system to a terrorist organization. There had been no public statements and no ultimatums. It was sheer nonsense. Most religious people had resigned themselves to the presence of abortion in society and decided that God should best punish the perpetrators in the afterlife.

The German High Ministry of Science soon declared that the second largest meteorite ever to strike the earth was the cause of the Sogink disaster. The statistical probability of this happening again in our lifetime was one in ten million. Berlin would rebuild and rise again. But the fire officials knew what the public did not. There was no physical evidence of a meteorite. There were no residual stones, chemicals or gases like those found at other meteorite crash zones. They were ordered by the Interior Ministry to keep this information confidential to avoid public hysteria. If they defied authority they would be considered enemies of the state. The fire marshall and the captain met for a beer. They were experienced firefighters. They had seen it all. They had both studied the results of World War II fire bombings and the incineration of Japanses cities by nuclear weapons. They knew what they had witnessed was paranormal. It was "hell-fire." Or, maybe, "angel-fire." Nothing that hot had ever been recorded on earth. They decided to privately consult university science department chairs. The Chancellor was secretly advised to put the home defense forces and radar units on full alert.

The members of the maintenance crews who had left Sogink for their auto job interviews praised God that they were away from the plant during the inferno. They firmly believed they were spared the heaven-sent fury because of their distaste for the product they were making. This was no accident of nature. This was a message from heaven. Stop. Stop the murder.

Within weeks, Dresden and Hamburg were running full-steam filling orders from around the world. They used crates of stock replacement parts to make pumps they would fully warranty. At an emergency Sogink board meeting the CEO reported they were quickly rebuilding the Berlin assembly plant and satisfying most orders in a timely manner. When Berlin was finished it would be more heavily guarded and completely fireproof. The other two facilities would switch back to warehousing. Customers they had satisfied for years were graciously sticking by them in this tragic time.

The following Sunday hundreds of workers filled the Dresden and Hamburg plants. They were on a 24/7 schedule now. The sky was quiet on the radar screens. At dusk white hot fireballs streaked across the northern sky and vaporized both facilities. The feuerwagen did little good. Again, there were no ruins and no body parts, just dirt. At the request of Germany the United Nations called an emergency meeting in New York City. The American President ordered the Joint Chiefs of Staff to find any possible terrorists. And in Rome, the Holy Father called a meeting of the College of Cardinals. The head of the OPF phoned Bishop Francisco and demanded he visit Monsignor Borgogno at his new post in the Florida seminary immediately. "This is your problem. Fix it."

"Yes, Your Eminence. It will be done."

Chapter 4

After another wickedly busy week in the largest women's clinic in Texas, Bill Sherwood counted and deposited his cash and decided to head to the marina for an overnight stay. He was happy to see the pink sunset from his private office window. "Red sky at night, sailor's delight." He asked his girlfriend, also the head nurse at the clinic, to spend the night and try an early cruise on Saturday. "Definitely" Nancy replied. The doctor called his wife and said the guys would crash on the boat to go fishing at dawn. He would be home by supper Saturday. He wanted to be alone with Nancy and thank her for moving all those cases through his office every week.

She had helped him build one of the largest termination centers in the South. No hassles. No 24-hour waiting period. No parental notification. They even thought of adding late-term services to make up for the doctor who was shot a few states away. Bill held off because the state's late-term ban was still before the courts. If the pro-lifers lost he would make his move. Like most Texas businessmen, he packed heat and wasn't afraid of local loudmouths.

Nancy was a stunning Latin-American beauty contest winner who had settled in Texas following nursing school. She was a smart nurse and dated fast and heavy. She had used the Sherwood clinic for "accidents" several times and jumped at the chance of a job opening. Soon she was promoted and took a fancy to the boss. She often volunteered to stay late to clean and began to discreetly date Doctor Bill. She was at his beck and call for fun nights on the boat and never demanded to be seen with him in public. He rewarded her with jewelry, a car and steamy sex. She also got a bonus based on the number of cases she managed at the clinic each week. His marriage did not bother her…that was his problem.

After a bottle of wine and soft-shell crabs the two spent a cozy night aboard Bill's new sloop *"Her Choice."* The sails and controls were electronic. He would have no problem skippering the 45 foot double-masted vessel with just a little help from his first mate. If the wind died he had a trusty diesel engine to get them home. The Saturday forecast called for calm seas with a 5-10 knot breeze out of the northwest. The barometer was rising. Highs in the 80's. All clear from NOAA weather radio. What a night! What a day to come!

At sunup he motored out the inlet and decided to tack upwind, eat lunch then take a lazy sail back to the marina. As usual when shorthanded, he would stay within sight of land. After an exciting two hours it was lunch time. The breezes calmed and Bill dropped the sails. Nancy had sandwiches and beer ready in the galley but before the meal she wanted a repeat of last night's performance in the stateroom as an appetizer. Later they took a quick swim, ate and planned to head back. The problem now was......no wind. No point hoisting any sails. He fired up the trusty diesel and headed home.

Bill noticed clouds developing in the north. The sky darkened and the temperature fell. With a sleek hull and strong engine they would beat the coming storm. If they had to, they could run for shore, beach the boat and set a land anchor. Suddenly, the engine quit. In his haste to cast off, and a little fuzzy from the wine, he had forgotten to check the fuel gauge in the morning. The clouds moved closer and the wind strengthened. He raised his jib sail to catch some of the new breeze and get the hell home. Then he saw it. The cold front hitting the stalled warm air mass had created a waterspout, a rotating funnel with strong winds and pouring rain. No hope of outrunning this. As it closed on them he began to hear the sucking noises and the sound of buzzing bees described by witnesses of ocean cyclones. He dropped the jib, threw out his storm anchor and took Nancy below. They slammed down the hatch and closed the portholes. They tried to pray but didn't know how.

The police and Coast Guard took statements from witnesses on the beach. The waterspout came from the north and went straight at the sailboat. The boat spun wildly and flipped side-to-side. The rigging blew away and the masts broke off. Then the small tornado disappeared straight up above the clouds. The rescue vessel arrived to find a ruined boat. The portholes were blown in. Below officers found the torsos of a man and woman. Their arms and legs had been ripped off their bodies and the expensive teak floor was red. Written in blood on the ceiling was the word "*STOP.*" News of this bizarre event spread like wildfire. People learned that the popular abortion doctor and his mistress had died by having their bodies ripped apart by a cyclone at sea.

The Archbishop of Canterbury invited the heads of the major world religions to London for an urgent meeting. He decried all forms of violence even that done in the name of justice. The Papal Secretariat summoned a convocation of Cardinals to study the issue and provide the Pope with the documents necessary to formulate an urgent encyclical. Roman officials were already in America studying the most recent incident. The head Rabbi of the World Jewish Congress likened the scourge of abortion to the vile Holocaust seventy years earlier. Maybe the God of the Old Testament had sent his revenge on the criminals of the twenty-first century. He predicted seven events or perhaps seven years of retribution in keeping with the seven lamps of the Temple Menorah.

The American President got no answers from his military and civilian leaders. They were stumped. There were religious marches and peace protests in all major cities. The women's lobby had powerful connections at the White House and they demanded something be done to protect abortion clinics. Attacks on equipment facilities and now a provider could greatly limit people's right to choose. The President reasoned these terrorist attacks had come from the sky and perhaps the only safe place to provide this healthcare would be in underground bunkers until they could find the perpetrators. He ordered the Secretaries of Defense and HHS to study the idea of setting up regional health clinics in big city air-raid shelters. If the constitution and the courts guaranteed the right to an abortion he felt obliged to provide locations around the country where women would be safe. He privately told his Cabinet that if abortions were to end there would clearly be insufficient funds for hospitals, welfare payments and food stamps for all the unwanted babies. The only option, perhaps, would be forced sterilization and that would never fly. Defense would prepare one shelter for every ten states and HHS would seek volunteer doctors to staff these facilities by the end of the month. In case of a doctor shortage, physicians from the Veteran's Administration would be trained and relocated to the centers. No one would be turned away for lack of funds.

Chapter 5

The sleek red and white Gulfstream jet landed at Fort Lauderdale airport on a hot afternoon. The assistant pastor of Our Lady, the Roman Catholic Cathedral, was waiting on the tarmac in the church limo. He had heard of, but never met, the Vatican delegate, Senior Bishop Francisco. "Welcome to Florida, Your Excellency. My Bishop sends his regards but is in hospital with a respiratory ailment or he would meet you himself. Please allow me to kiss your ring."

"Very well. Sorry to hear about Bishop Mark. Please send him my condolences. Have you arranged for Boynton Beach?"

"Yes, Your Excellency. We are 37 miles from the seminary. St. Vincent is a beautiful school. It opened in 1963 and serves all seven dioceses of Florida. It is bilingual and graduates 25 priests with masters degrees every year. I hear your recent appointee, Monsignor Borgogno, has become quite a hit already."

"I will need lodging and a private meeting room to discuss official Church business."

"Of course, Bishop. Now for a nice ride and some refreshments."

That week Matthew Edwards had received a letter summoning him to Florida. Enclosed was a one-way ticket to Fort Lauderdale airport for Saturday morning. After Friday night's catechism class he packed his bag and was told a parishioner would drive him in the early morning to the local airport. His pastor knew all about it. "See you whenever, Matthew. Good luck!"

"Yes, Monsignor, thank you."

The Bishop met Borgogno and Edwards in the large private office of the seminary dean. It was the weekend and the school was empty. Seniors were on a bus trip visiting churches in the local parishes to see where they might be assigned after graduation. The rest were given time off to go to the beach. A butler delivered the prepared lunch and left the room. "Now, we all know each other from St. Michael's. Everyone was impressed by the hard work and piety of both of you. And I'm sure you've been pretty happy with your subsequent assignments?"

"Yes, Your Excellency," they both said.

"Matthew, do you like being in a nice church in your hometown?"

"Yes, sir, definitely."

"And Monsignor, I hear you've been well-received at this beautiful seminary by the beach?"

"Yes, Bishop, I like it here."

"If you both wish to maintain your good standing, you must help me. Whatever you did in Rome, it seems you started serious trouble." The old man became agitated and red-faced. "My superiors in Rome demand I put an end to this. The Pontiff is an old man and not too healthy. He has traveled the world preaching peace and love. I can tell you from close personal friends he is not happy with this. If it gets out that your little summer session had something to do with a new religious jihad it could be worse PR for us than the abuse scandal! We were supposed to pray for peace. But you.... you had to start World War III. Now, my direct superior has instructed me that you are to regroup and pray for the cessation of hostilities. Do you understand?"

"Bishop, over the past few weeks I have been shocked by the developments in Germany and America. But I never really thought it had anything to do with us. Who is it that believes this? Why would God or his Angels listen to a lowly group of priests? And you know, if this destruction has come from the right hand of God, how could we stop it? Perhaps this is the only way political leaders will put an end to the murderous practice of abortion."

"John, of course the Holy Father would prefer abstinence or even contraception to abortion, but he can't promote that. Besides, if unborn babies die their souls go to heaven, where you and I hope to go someday. Think about it. We can't stop sex and it seems we can't stop the private activities of a woman and her doctor. But we can stop you and your renegade band of violent warriors. Consider it an order of the Vatican Secretariat to reassemble your prayer group as soon as possible at this school. Make up a new prayer. Say it was all a misunderstanding. Call off the attacks. Catholics are peace-loving. The Jews of the Old Testament were the hateful ones, calling down floods and plagues. There is no room for that in our religion any longer. You will be given a dormitory wing with a chapel and cafeteria. Rome wishes the near- panic gripping the world to end. What a plus it will be for our Church when everyone finds out that *we* made the killing stop…. not the Protestants or the Jews. I guarantee each of you will be promoted and given choice assignments. This is the will of my direct superior whose name I can't reveal. I'm sure he will lead the Church one day. And if you choose to disobey his order, you will both have a taste of hell on earth. Let me be blunt. There are rumors around the Vatican about the Monsignor who was transferred all over the U.S. and is now traveling with a good-looking young priest! I'm sure your conscience is clear, Borgogno, but the press is always looking for new gossip. Lawyers and politicians are trying to cash in on the gravy train, suck money out of our collection baskets. You have stirred up tremendous anguish throughout the world with your scheme. If this is not rectified, well…..it could get unpleasant. So, if your group has some weird influence with the Angels or Saints, pray this ends. You belong to a religious society, not a democratic one. This is an order. FIX IT! NOW! Do I make myself clear?"

"Your Excellency, whatever happens, please don't hold this against young Matthew. He opposed it from the beginning. It was my misguided sense of justice that has, perhaps, caused this pain. I shall reconvene the Institute for Focused Prayer and attempt to put an end to the destruction. But Bishop, we might not be successful. It may be God's plan that a few more events happen to scare people. No one knows God's will. But be assured that we shall obey you and fervently pray to the Angels as you desire." Francisco tossed a book on the table and Borgogno began phoning the senior proctors from the program at St. Michael's. They would all arrive by Monday. The Bishop would stay a few days to ensure they were following his orders.

Francisco retired for a nap and the Monsignor rode a bicycle to a nearby service station with a private old-fashioned phone booth. He summoned the long-distance operator to place a collect call for him to Italy. "Hello, Miguel? How are you, my friend? Thank you for taking my call. Your humble servant pleads with you for a massive favor. I need you to pose a question to *HIM*. How does HE feel about my activities? I am in an impossible predicament. Only *HE* can guide me. Does *HE* want this all to stop....or continue?" The old Monsignor from Argentina welcomed John's call and said he would try to provide some guidance as quickly as possible. He warned Borgogno to be cautious and praised his valor. Borgogno gave his old friend Matthew's cell phone number.

On Monday the twelve small groups met for a mass celebrated by the Bishop. It was September 29, the feast of St. Michael the Archangel! In the homily the Bishop asked the convocation to pray to Michael to protect them. He finished with the liturgical prayer of

St. Michael's feastday: "Oh God, who dost establish the ministry of Angels and men in a wonderful order, graciously grant that Thy holy Angels, whoever serve Thee in heaven, may also protect our lives on earth. Your Bishop servant humbly asks you, Father, to listen to the voices of the congregation gathered here as we pray for an end to the destruction of our cities and people."

After mass the Bishop decided to have a car drive him to breakfast at the beach while the others began to focus on the job at hand. Borgogno had the young priests dine alone while he met with the seniors. "What do you think my fellow leaders? What shall we do? Did any of you feel the same courage and power in Francisco's sermon as we felt every day at St. Michael's? If we have the ear of the Archangel, should we pray for him to stop or is the world truly about to change? Will the Angel end abortion the way the Allied invasion ended the holocaust? If we pray against the wishes of our superior I can tell you we may all personally suffer. He might leave the youngsters alone but not us. Our flaws might be revealed and who has no faults? But what is right? Please think this over today and tomorrow we shall gather in the chapel and raise our voices to God, one way or the other."

The next morning, as Borgogno prepared for early mass, he saw several airport taxis leaving the courtyard. At the chapel he noticed some of the groups had departed. There were rumors that many of the old padres could not bear the stress of facing outlandish charges. Some had become ill and left messages with the Bishop's secretary that they supported his position and would pray privately in their home churches for world peace. At the chapel, seven pairs remained, one from each continent. Borgogno addressed the group: "I have considered the risk to myself and I see the Lord's hand now at work in the world. I believe we should pray for Michael to continue his work. However, I understand this is just my thinking. We need to come to a democratic decision here. I have asked a well-placed friend to obtain supreme guidance for us but this may be impossible."

Various opinions were expressed by the devout men gathered in the pews. Most did not believe that their actions would really make a difference. Perhaps they should all beg their leave of the Bishop and assure him of their support. They had no authority to do otherwise. Maybe enough had been done by the Archangel to set the world straight. If they only had some higher advice. Matthew then felt the silenced phone begin to vibrate in his shirt pocket. "Monsignor! A text!" He jumped up and went quickly to the pulpit.

Borgogno's face lit up with the green light of the smart phone's screen. He read the message to his friends: "Pater imploro persevero, etiam medicina!" ("Leader asks to continue, also medicine!").

The Monsignor had heard that many abortions in the world were now below the radar screen, unseen in the large city clinics. In the late 1980s, drugs were developed in Europe that could terminate a pregnancy in its first few months. Only women and their doctors would know about it. Some companies and governments fought the release of these drugs but others promoted them. It was estimated that in America twenty-five percent of the abortions were now carried out with these killing medicines. In Europe and Asia the numbers were up to seventy percent. Over time, the boards of directors of some companies ordered their management to stop producing these pills or at least sell off the patents. Currently, most of these medicines were being produced in France and China. Some of the patents were owned by Sogink!

Encouraged by the text message, the group decided to continue praying to the Angels to stop abortion. "Archangel Metatron, scribe and overseer of the Angels, the children of God ask you to send us Michael, the conquerer of Lucifer....... Michael, warrior, protector of heaven, come to us and save the souls of the unborn......Do as you must to redeem these slaughtered souls......Destroy the means of destruction....We ask this in God's holy name. Amen."

At Fort Lauderdale airport the Bishop's red and white jet was ready for takeoff. The mild air turbulence reported to the cockpit by the tower would be no problem for this magnificent aircraft. Only the largest businesses and a few international charities could afford to own and maintain a jet like this. It had a crew of three and seating for 12 passengers. There was a galley and a small office with a fax machine and satellite communications. Travel range was 7,000 miles. The Bishop notified his superior that his mission was accomplished. A week of prayers for world peace was beginning in Florida that would surely satisfy his wishes. After takeoff he would have lunch and settle in for a smooth flight to Italy.

VJ123 received clearance for departure and left the hanger for the longest runway on the private side of the airport. It would head northeast over Bermuda and set a course to the continent. The sky darkened and clouds were rolling in as the captain prepared for takeoff. They were airborne and over the ocean in ten seconds. Heavy wind gusts shook the jet as the pilot tried to rise above the cloud cover. On the beach, lifeguards were signaling surfers to paddle back to shore as someone had spotted a waterspout on the horizon. The sky was suddenly black.

A Coast Guard patrol boat was dispatched after the windstorm and spotted the wreckage of VJ123, still on the surface due to its excellent flotation. Crewmen in life jackets swam inside the cabin. The doors and windows had been torn off. They found blood and body parts and on the ceiling scrawled in red: "*STOP.*" The lieutenant in charge radioed for a larger ship to haul in the wreckage and noted in his log: "Probable in-flight accident causing loss of altitude, possibly due to collision with birds." The master wrote in his diary: "Another Bermuda triangle mystery. Can't believe it didn't sink.... like somebody wanted us to find it!"

In Shanghai, engineers and common laborers rode bicycles through the factory gate. Most of the workers wore facemasks because of the smog. They worked twelve hour shifts to produce most of the abortion drugs for Asia and the Americas. In the basement of the large factory there were showers and cots. The accommodations were better than in most homes. Employees would often spend a week at the plant picking up extra hours when they could. In Lyon, people arrived by scooters and small cars to work around the clock filling orders for similar medications to be distributed throughout Europe and Africa. At midnight yellow-white fireballs shot out of the skies above Shanghai and Lyon vaporizing the two plants.

Chapter 6

In Washington, the Cabinet was ordered to develop an options list for the administration. They settled on a plan to set up regional women's health centers – five for now–Boston, Philadelphia, Atlanta, Chicago and San Francisco. Most were in underground settings. All would be protected by small surface-to-air missile/radar units in National Guard trucks. The centers' roofs would be fitted with heavy reflecting tiles to repel any possible laser attacks. Bus routes to outlying cities would be established to bring patients to the clinics on Mondays, Wednesdays and Fridays for a start. Insurance would be accepted and coverage made mandatory by an executive order of the President.

In New York, the UN General Assembly was summoned for an historic deliberation. The five permanent members of the Security Council met in a soundproof room with only their personal assistants present. It was hoped they would come to a unanimous consensus on the issues of mass violence and abortion rights. They could then speak in a unified voice in the General Assembly on how to proceed. Instead, the ambassadors from three of the nations had been ordered to stand by their countries' laws allowing abortion. The Chinese saw overpopulation as a major threat in the coming century. Already they had outlawed more than one child per family. Also, they produced half of the medicines used in the world for abortions and these profits were critical. The American administration was too beholden to women's rights groups and other liberal backers to change their stance at this time. Likewise, the French government was an active promoter of abortions and part-owner of the Lyon pharmaceutical plant that had just been destroyed. The nation was solidly pro-choice.

The Russians worried about their declining population. Twenty-five percent of Russian men were now dying by age fifty-five from drinking and other vices. The government had done everything it could to encourage families to have two or three children but still suffered a negative growth rate. Perhaps outlawing abortion...... easier in a totalitarian state than in a democracy...... would be a partial remedy. Finally, in London, the Queen and the government had met with the Archbishop of Canterbury and decided to issue a ban on all abortions in the United Kingdom as well as travel by her subjects outside the UK for such action. The Archbishop had informed the Queen of his recent dream about the Angel of Death visiting the homes of world leaders who would not support the abolition of abortion. How many children might be sacrificed for this unholy activity? The Queen's decree was of the highest royal order and could not be overridden by Parliament.

That night the British ambassador to the UN addressed the General Assembly: "Her Majesty, the Queen, wishes to convey to all people of the world our desire for peace and freedom and an end to violence in all its forms…… including the scourge of abortion. We must promote sound moral upbringing, good health care and affordable contraception. But life…..is life. We all know it when we see it on a small ultrasound screen. It's time to stop the denial. It's time to stop the killing. We ask the delegates in the General Assembly to support a worldwide ban on medical and surgical abortions. We propose extra funding for education and contraception throughout the civilized world and we will be the first nation to contribute one billion pounds to this cause. Woe to the nations who will not follow us in this righteous endeavor." The Russian ambassador grabbed his microphone to quickly endorse the British proposal. Half of the Assembly rose in loud applause.

Next to speak was the US ambassador. Her assistant loaded the prepared remarks into a teleprompter. She had been the President's phone secretary at his mayoral office then his legislative assistant in Congress. After his meteoric rise, she was given the UN ambassador position as a gift but had no foreign policy experience and was not an accomplished public speaker. "Mr. Secretary General, Honorable Delegates, Ladies and Gentlemen: Welcome to New York, USA, the land of the free and the home of the brave. We cherish our liberty.

We've fought hard for over two centuries for civil rights. We will protect the rights of all women in the voting booth, in the workplace and in doctors' offices. Through God-given gains in science and technology, researchers around the world have discovered ways for women to safeguard their health and their reproductive choices. We will not abandon them now because of some perverse attempts to destroy the industries that provide women with these critical technologies. Our intelligence officials believe that radical right-wing extremists have gained control of some cutting-edge weaponry to rob women of their choices and force them back into kitchens and bedrooms. My President pledges to eliminate these terrorists. I announce tonight that any nation requesting our assistance to protect health care facilities will be given financial and defensive military aid to ensure that their citizens enjoy the same rights as Americans. Our Secretaries of Defense and HHS will set up working groups with all UN member nations to begin this process. Do not be fooled. The recent attacks were not heavenly warnings but rather religious fanaticism. Stay strong. We are with you in this struggle." Her remarks, though not her own, were eloquent and well-received. They had not been shared in advance with Congress. Bipartisan leaders of the House and Senate had requested a meeting with the President prior to this important address. The President's chief of staff notified them that the boss was too busy to schedule a briefing and felt that he had the executive authority to offer the world a new abortion security blanket in the form of a treaty which he would allow the Senate to review ninety days after its emergency implementation.

The French delegate rose in the noisy hall to endorse the American plan, defending against the recent assaults on basic freedoms. However, due to the state of his economy, they would be unable to contribute to this "health and welfare fund." The Chinese ambassador proclaimed the recent hostile attacks would ultimately bring the Chinese and American people closer together. But, his nation reserved the right to strike back at the point of origin of the deadly missiles wherever that might be. Their military was now developing response plans.

The Secretary-General was unable to establish order in the Assembly Hall. He banged the gavel then flashed the lights to no avail. Half of the delegates had split off to one side to greet the British and Russian delegates while the others signed documents requesting American aid. Joined by her French and Chinese counterparts, the U.S. ambassador urged all governments to be strong in resisting the foes of abortion. Frustrated, the UN leader walked off the stage and headed to his limousine. The Assembly was hopelessly divided.

In the sweltering heat of the little Florida chapel members of the reconstituted Institute for Focused Prayer called on God's Angels to continue their activities. Political leaders would have to be convinced of the immorality of abortion. Borgogno proposed they stay for a week of prayer then return to their home countries for pastoral duties. Time would tell if their mission was successful. In the morning he would preside over the funeral mass for Bishop Ignatius Francisco. The Bishop had no immediate family and it was decided to bury his remains in the small cemetery at St. Vincent Seminary guarded by a statue of Michael the Archangel.

After supper Matthew Edwards approached the Monsignor with a buzzing cell phone. It was Monsignor Miguel. The British government, represented by the Archbishop of Canterbury, had asked for a full briefing on the activities of the Institute. The Holy Father himself requested someone from Florida be sent to London for this purpose. Miguel asked Borgogno "If you cannot go, whom do you trust for this task?"

"It will be my personal assistant, Father Edwards, my friend. He can leave in the morning."

"Very well. The Archbishop's car will be at Heathrow when he arrives. He must answer all the government's questions and give them the conclave's recommendations. God bless you all."

"Yes, my friend, thank you."

The next evening Matthew dined at 10 Downing Street with the Prime Minister, the Foreign Minister, the Archbishop and some staffers. He told them how their project had begun and, though never explicitly stated, he always felt he had support at the highest levels of the Catholic Church for their summer conclave. It seems, perhaps, they had stirred sleeping Angels who brought down the wrath of the Old Testament. They had begun to rid the world of the genocide that was so routine today. It may have been unrelated to their prayers. It may have just been God's time for retribution. Those in Florida were unsure what would happen next especially if the powerful nations did not make quick plans to end abortion and set an example for the developing countries. The priests at the Institute believed that the sooner nations officially banned abortion the quicker the Angel of Death would be satisfied. They had read the British plan, proposed at the UN, and strongly endorsed it. He left his cell phone number and offered any further consultation they might require. He would stay for the weekend at the rectory of St. Peter's Italian Church then return to Florida. The Archbishop asked Matthew if he might recite the prayer developed in Rome that had been so powerful. "Do you have it with you, son?"

"Sir, of course, I know it by heart. I wrote it!" Matthew had everyone at the table join hands. Some of them trembled as an energy seemed to course through their bodies while listening to the young American's prayer. A few gasped in amazement. The Archbishop requested Matthew join them in the morning for a special service at the central London Cathedral. He wanted his parishioners to hear this prayer to inspire them and help them understand the Queen's recent order ending abortion in the UK.

In the morning the central London Cathedral was overflowing. Some were joyous, others scared. Rumors had surfaced of a powerful American priest coming to give a sermon on recent events. Silently the Archbishop, in splendid garments, processed in with all his attendants. Matthew followed, awed by the enormity of the place. He had never been in such a large church, let alone preach to this big a crowd. After opening prayers, there were two Scripture readings by the chief deacon. The first was an account of John the Baptist from Matthew 3:7: "You brood of vipers....the one who will follow me.... will baptize you in the Holy Spirit and fire.....His winnowing-fan is in his hand. He will clear the threshing floor and gather his grain into the barn, but the chaff he will burn in unquenchable fire." The second reading, of hope and faith, was taken from Isaiah 12:1: "...on that day you will sing: I give you thanks, oh Lord; though you have been angry with me, your anger has abated, and you have consoled me. God indeed is my Savior; I am confident and unafraid."

The Archbishop gestured for Matthew to take the pulpit. Shaking a bit, he climbed the four steps and pulled out his notes. He looked out over the quiet crowd. He noticed in the back of the Cathedral the small red light on the BBC camera. "Archbishop, distinguished clergy, ladies and gentlemen, today I bring you words of caution and of hope. Many have prayed for the end of abortion. This sin is as serious as any other in history. We live in a time when no one accepts personal responsibility for his actions. We blame other people or our situation in life for the things we do wrong. I believe the time for personal responsibility has come; responsibility for individuals, for evildoers and for the leaders of sinful nations. I am not here asking anyone to become Catholic or to change their beliefs. I am here to plead for the killing to stop. Listen to the biblical warnings of both

Testaments. In Romans 1:18: 'The wrath of God is being revealed from heaven against the irreligious and perverse spirit of men..... They are filled with every kind of wickedness: maliciousness, greed, ill will, envy, murder....They know God's just decree that all who do such things deserve death; yet they not only do them but approve them in others.' From Isaiah13: 'I have commanded my dedicated soldiers, I have summoned my warriors, eager and bold to carry out my anger. Listen! The rumble on the mountains....Listen, nations assembled! The Lord of hosts is mustering an army for battle. They come from a far-off country, and from the end of the heavens... to lay waste the land and destroy the sinners within it....Thus I will punish the world for its evil and the wicked for their guilt.' Again from Isaiah 42: 'So he poured out wrath upon them, yet they did not realize, it burned them, but they took it not to heart.' "

"Our former Pope, Benedict XVI declared in 2011: 'Society as a whole must defend the conceived child's right to life and the true good of the woman who can never, in any circumstances, find fulfillment in the decision to abort.' In our monastery we prayed for God to deliver his people from the scourge of abortion, forty million of them yearly .We prayed to the Archangels. It is written in Daniel 12:1: '.... at that time shall arise Michael, the great prince who has charge of your people. And there shall be a time of trouble such as never has been since there was a nation until that time.' We pleaded with God to send the instruments of his wrath to cleanse us of our wickedness. They are here. Will we listen and pay heed? Here is our prayer." As Matthew began, the rising sun shone through the large stained glass windows behind the altar. First the pulpit then the whole church was bathed in amber light. "Dear God, almighty Father, creator of the universe, hear us. Listen to your servants as we pray to you. Lord, your people need your intervention. We beseech you to stop the slaughter of the innocents. We deplore the loss of millions of souls that long to be with you in heaven. Your faithful children have prayed for decades to overturn the injustice of this immoral act but have been unsuccessful. We turn to you now to stop the genocide. Let loose your Angels. Send them down from heaven to fight this atrocity with your righteous vengeance."

"Archangel Metatron, scribe and overseer of the Angels, the children of God ask you to send us Michael, the conqueror of Lucifer. The satanic forces at work in our land can only be overcome by the same God-given power used to drive Satan into hell. Michael, warrior, protector of heaven, come to us and save the souls of the unborn. Thousands of years ago God sent floods, pestilence, and the Angel of Death to the firstborn of the Egyptians to save his people and establish His dominion on the earth. Do as you must to redeem these slaughtered souls for the Father, the Son and the Holy Spirit. We ask this in God's holy name. Amen."

Matthew thanked the congregation for their attention and their government for its willingness to address this issue. "My superiors in the U.S. and Rome thank you for your support as we continue our efforts to end abortion. I know we shall be successful as we have God and his holy Angels on our side." As he finished the light in the Cathedral windows became brilliant gold. People felt their pews shake and heard the sound of distant trumpets. But there was no choir today and there were no instruments. Matthew grabbed the pulpit railing and felt a mild shock. The Archbishop realized they were having a "peak experience," described as an ecstatic state of euphoria possessing a mystical and spiritual quality. In these exciting moments, people have described intense feelings of well-being and awe and some have levitated. This state comes on suddenly and is usually inspired by deep meditation. The congregation rose. There were chants and some screams.

The leader of the world Anglican Church and his London Bishops were stunned. The Archbishop canceled the Eucharistic half of the service as people were streaming out the doors. He advised Matthew to have the church limo out back take him to St. Peter's rectory. A large crowd had gathered in the front yard of the Cathedral. News vans cut off the driveway, filming the gold light shining out of the doors and windows. When Matthew approached the Archbishop's car, he was confronted by pro-choice and union demonstrators. "There's the American warmonger who has called for attacks on our rights and our factories. Let's give him a warm European welcome!" They began shoving the young priest as he reached for the car door. Before he could get in the back seat he was struck with heavy placards in the stomach and back. The driver pulled him in by his coat sleeve and quickly drove away knocking down some of the thugs. "Could you please take me to St. Peter's rectory, sir?"

"Nonsense, lad, I'm retired army and you've taken enough shots to deserve a medical exam. We're going to St. George's Hospital. It has a great emergency department and over 1300 beds if you need to be put in." The driver radioed the Archbishop's office which sent a police car and a detachment from the Foreign Ministry to the hospital.

Half of the ER ramp was cordoned off by men in bulging black sport coats. Matthew was taken to a secure cubicle in a wheelchair. "So, you're the famous American priest? I'm Doctor Williams and this is Nurse Malin. How do you feel?"

"Pretty good, Doctor, considering. I need to get back to St. Peter's rectory and then to Florida quickly."

"Well, we hear you've taken some hard blows. British hospitality! We'll give you a quick checkup and get some labs then release you if we can. Rumor has it you brought on some sort of mystical trance at the Cathedral so perhaps you're invincible…..your stay should be short!"

"News travels fast," Matthew exclaimed.

"I'm told your bag has been brought 'round from St. Peter's. If we can clear you, your car will go directly to Heathrow for a flight to the States tonight. The pilot is on standby."

"His history is clean, Doctor. No illness, no smoking, no medicines and no allergies. The only surgery was a right-sided kidney donation to his younger brother. That scar seems to be well-healed."

"Thank you, nurse. Let's get some blood and a urine specimen. His exam here is fairly negative. A few scrapes and bruises, nothing serious, but make the labs stat."

"Oui."

"Thank you, nurse." In thirty minutes Doctor Paul Williams and Nurse Marie Malin came back to Matthew's cubicle. "Father Edwards, your chemistries were all fine but I'm afraid there's one problem. You have blood in your urine!"

"Is that serious, Doctor?"

"I hope not, but we need to check for any damage to your remaining kidney. You took a good shot to your back. It's only a trace of blood so I think you're okay but you need a total body Cat scan for safety. I'll arrange for it immediately. And, you know, Father, you have a lot of people praying for you. Malin, can you start an IV?"

"Oui, Doctor." Malin had gone into nursing for the power and the excitement. She was not particularly sympathetic to the ill and did not need the money. Malin came from a family of wealthy pharmaceutical executives who had just lost one of their factories in Lyon! She was a transplant to England, sent by the directors to watch over some of their business interests in London. She dabbled in nursing part-time. The nurse roughly pushed Matthew's arm down for an IV. As she jabbed at him she whispered: "I know about you, Mr. Edwards. I've never been a zealot but I believe in reproductive rights. Here in England I have always kept my mouth shut but I can no longer be silent. I must speak out against the damage you and your Church have done. And now, you've killed my brother. He ran the medicine plant in Lyon that you had destroyed. I hate you! I hope you die in this hospital…..but it won't be at my hand. I'm too religious for that. But you, you are evil" she finished, weeping. Malin walked to the nurse's break room and scrolled through the contacts in her cell phone. She selected 'IE' for the Italian Embassy and pushed "dial." A few seconds later she whispered "He's here!" She was told to keep Edwards there for an hour at all costs. Someone would be sent. She went back to his cubicle but he was gone.

An orderly and a policeman wheeled Matthew's stretcher to Radiology. Because of his previous nephrectomy, he was given only half the usual dose of contrast dye which still seemed to make all the blood in his body burn. The motorized Cat scan table pushed him through the circular ring of x-ray cameras, back and forth. In fifteen minutes he was back in the ER and felt a great urge to visit the bathroom. Matthew decided it might not be safe to stay there much longer. He washed and dressed and sized up the window in the bathroom for a quick escape. He couldn't be sure if the doctor or the guards were on his side. He knew the nurse was not. He would slide out the window and catch a taxi to the airport. Surely the Archbishop would alert the standby pilot of his arrival.

"Father Edwards, you in there? Are you okay?" It was Doctor Williams. "Please come out. We must talk." Matthew felt a sense of calm and unlocked the bathroom door. "The Archbishop's driver is waiting in the rear to take you to Heathrow. I'll push you out in a wheelchair covered with an overcoat. I want you to get safely to Florida or Rome or wherever they send you. I believe in your mission. You are a very blessed and lucky man. I've never heard of this "peak experience" you caused today but my parents were there and said you restored their faith in God."

"Thank you, Doctor Williams, but I can't take credit for that. It just happened."

"I don't know what to believe, about this or life in general. I was a devout Anglican but what I saw as a para-medic in Afghanistan made me question my whole belief system. I don't know what to do. I came back to medical school and now I'm in the ER but I just seem to be drifting."

"You're not drifting, Doctor. You are answering God's call. You're a healer….and a good one. Do your best every day and be kind along the way. That's what God wants for you."

"Well, I know something magical happened today and I think you'll remember it for the rest of your life. Before you go, listen to your Cat scan report. 'FINDINGS of stat total body contrast CT of ER patient Rev. Matthew Edwards: #1. No obvious fractures of the four extremities #2. No evidence of significant skull or intra-cranial injury. #3. Mild contusions of the subcutaneous thoracic tissues-anterior and posterior- with no significant pulmonic injury. #4. The heart, great vessels, liver and spleen are normal without evidence of bleeding. There is no free fluid noted in the chest or abdominal cavities. The intestines are intact. There is no free air #5. Both kidneys appear normal and excrete dye to the bladder within accepted time parameters. IMPRESSION: Normal total body CT study. Historical data regarding previous unilateral nephrectomy appears to be incorrect.' I phoned my friend in Radiology. Two kidneys, Father! There was no mix up. It's you. Something incredible has happened my friend....you got a reward for your hard work. I had your report copied. Take it along and Godspeed to you."

"I can't believe it. Thank you. Thank you so much. Can I get out of here?" In five minutes Matthew got into the church limo waiting at the basement loading dock. He thanked the driver for bringing him to St. George's that day. On his way to the airport, Matthew read the Cat scan report then slept all the way across the Atlantic on his first private jet trip ......aboard the red and white VJ111..... to Florida.

At St. Vincent's Monsignor Borgogno was winding down the weeklong seminar. Matthew described the events at the Cathedral and the emotional and physical results of the "peak experience." He felt the United Kingdom was solidly behind them. Adding the power of the Vatican might be enough to sway the U.S. to prohibit abortion. Many smaller nations, dependent on American foreign aid, could follow suit. "Funny you should mention that, Matthew. Don't unpack. We're taking that jet back to Rome tomorrow! The others will finish up here while you and I get special instructions."

The next day the Archbishop phoned the Queen to tell of the recurrence of his terrible dream about the Angel of Death. He must notify the heads of the pro-abortion Security Council nations. Perhaps they would accept a temporary ban on the procedures and take some time to reconsider their stand at the UN. The Queen agreed and asked the Archbishop to proceed to the Foreign Ministry. There he phoned the Americans, French and the Chinese on their respective "hot lines." The Archbishop told his dreams and fears to each of the officials. The French would take the warning under advisement and consult with a special committee of Parliament. However, their President was known to be a strong advocate of abortion and the Foreign Minister doubted his mind could be swayed. Besides, the palace was heavily guarded in these troubled times. The Foreign Office in Beijing had been ordered by the President and the Central Committee to reiterate their support for abortion and announced their offer to match the educational and military funding of the Americans. In Washington, the Secretary of State told the Archbishop that he would relay the message to the President but could not guarantee a rapid response. He was sure the President appreciated the hard work of the British people and their government to secure world peace.

Later that week the Archbishop of Canterbury awoke with a fever and chills. He notified his secretary she would have to call 'round for a replacement minister for the day. A short time later she buzzed him with a phone call. It was the Prime Minister. "Archbishop, have you seen the news on the tele?"

"No, Prime Minister, I've caught a bit of a cold and cannot rise just yet."

"Sorry, sir, but you best have a look and call me back on the private line."

"Yes, Minister."

Live feeds to the BBC from Washington, Paris and Beijing were reporting on the tragic deaths of the youngest child of the American, French and Chinese Presidents. They had all lived at home and were found asphyxiated in their beds after apparent seizures. The screen flashed "A New Passover?" The BBC's senior correspondent in Washington opened: "7 AM in Washington, noon in London. We are reporting on the tragic deaths of the youngest children of the heads of state of three of the world's largest countries, all from apparent epileptic seizures. Also, there are rumors that these events were foretold by the Archbishop of Canterbury in dreams. The nightmares were relayed 'round the world through diplomatic channels but his warnings were summarily dismissed. Now these Presidents.... these abortion proponents.... these fathers.... realize the severity of the situation at hand. I can tell you here in Washington crowds are gathering at the White House gate. Some are placing candles at a makeshift memorial to the President's daughter. Others are carrying signs reading "ABORTION BEGETS DEATH!" Truly shocking. In London the Prime Minister announced he will ask the Archbishop to schedule an urgent meeting with world leaders and the heads of major religions on how to proceed. This was proposed some time ago but never came off. We've also learned of the Queen's offer of Windsor Castle, her 900 year old weekend retreat, for the proposed international gathering. This certainly thrusts Her Majesty's government into the forefront of the issue.

Reid Cameron was a seasoned political reporter who had won his share of broadcasting awards. He was one of the world's most respected broadcast journalists and was rumored to be in line for a coveted TV news anchor spot in London. His weekly BBC reports reached more than 150 million people. He had covered the horrors of war and could easily see through politicians' lies. But the religious overtones of this story frightened him.

"We'll sign out for now and send you back to BBC studios in London.....Hold on!......Hold on! This just in: we're getting reports that heavy storms across the U.S. overnight, many with violent lightning strikes, have knocked out power in the five new government–run abortion clinics stretching from Boston to San Francisco. There is no word of casualties but there were fires in the transformer rooms of those facilities. It seems all the electric outlets and new equipment were fried. How and where the Americans can continue to provide abortion – on demand is a bit uncertain at the moment. You have to imagine it'll be pretty hard to find an abortion doctor out in the open for a while. Scary stuff! The President's press secretary just announced the government is hastily reviewing all available video tapes from the White House grounds and the five national health clinics searching for evidence on these attacks. In all my decades reporting I have never seen anything like this. People of the world, you have to ask yourselves: can all this be due to random terrorism? We are left to wonder in amazement. We'll bring you up to date from Paris and Beijing next. Back to BBC headquarters for now."

Chapter 7

Aboard VJ111 the Monsignor and Matthew discussed the shocking developments they had seen on TV while packing for the flight. "What do you think will happen in those three countries, Monsignor?"

"Not sure, Matthew. We'll have to see how it plays out. I think we'll see some changes. I'm hoping for international guidance at the upcoming Windsor conference. Perhaps we'll have some discussion about that in Rome this week too. Maybe we'll be sent back as delegates to London."

"Maybe you, Monsignor, not me. It would be too presumptuous for me to consider that."

"You never know."

"Any chance this whole thing could get derailed now?"

"Well, nothing's guaranteed. There are powerful forces of evil at work in the world, often in sheep's clothing. Abortion satisfies the lustful and financial needs of human beings......murder for convenience."

The security guard who accompanied the pair on the flight to Rome, the kind with a bulging sport coat, had an earpiece and spoke to the captain several times as they approached Italy. The burly Tomaso had been a private investigator but didn't have the brains to make it in the business. He found a job as a personal guard at the travel office of the Vatican. Matthew thought Tomaso was wearing a bullet-proof vest. He definitely saw a shoulder holster. "Monsignor," the guard said," we will be landing shortly. You will be taken by car to meet with a high official at the Palace of the Holy Offices. As you may know, the palace was built in the 1920's to house major doctrinal centers of the Church. It's located just to the south of St. Peter's Basilica at the entrance to Vatican City. My boss runs it. You will have food and meetings have been arranged. You will be accompanied by several members of the Papal Swiss Guard.....for your protection."

The Swiss Guard is the oldest active military unit in existence. It was founded as a group of bodyguards for European royals in the late 1400's, first deployed in France in 1497. The original Pontifical Swiss Guard of the Holy See was established in Rome in 1506 under Pope Julius II. They developed a reputation for discipline, loyalty and up-to-date battle tactics. In 1874, an amendment to the Swiss constitution forbade foreign recruitment of Swiss Guards, but soldiers were allowed to volunteer for duty until 1927. All that remains of this 500-year-old institution is the Papal unit with 135 soldiers. Their job is the safety of the Pope and the security of the Apostolic

Palace. New recruits are sworn in every May. Their oath is recited in German.

A black limousine drove the pair and their plainclothes guard to the Palace of the Holy Offices. They were followed closely by an open Jeep with two Swiss Guards in their striped uniforms of blue, red, orange and yellow. Both wore black berets and carried swords….as well as semi-automatic Glocks! In the Jeep were their halberds, the traditional six foot long pole weapons topped with an axe blade and spike. Borgogno thought their destination was a bit unusual. He had expected some type of meeting at the Apostolic Palace which houses official government offices of the Church and the Holy See as well as chapels and museums. Also strange were the Swiss Guards. They're commonly deployed near the Pope's apartments and offices, not at the other palaces! He had trained here and knew the layout. Something was wrong.

The limousine drove through a rear gate of the palace. The two Swiss Guards accompanied them to a lower level office and opened a heavy door then stood at attention outside. Matthew sat in a comfortable lounge chair until the inner door opened and they were greeted by a portly man in the unmistakable black cassock and scarlet sash of a Cardinal. Hans Cardinal Khronin was a senior member of the College of Cardinals. He did not represent a specific archdiocese but rather had been the long-time director of a department of the Roman Curia responsible for doctrinal formulation. At his side was Tomaso. "Gentlemen, how was your trip?"

"Wonderful, Your Eminence, thank you." Both knelt as the Cardinal put his hands on their heads. Then they kissed the gold ring given to him by the Pope at his appointment.

"Let's have some refreshments," he said as waiters rolled in several trays from the kitchen.

"Your Eminence, to what do we owe this honor?"

"Well, Monsignor, I thought you might like a trip on my personal jet. A little bigger than the one that went down near the Bermuda triangle with my friend Francisco on board." The Cardinal dismissed the waiters but Tomaso stayed. Khronin became visibly upset. "The Bishop and I were very close, believed in the same causes. We went way back….to when the German-Italian alliance nearly dominated the world. Our fathers were recognized military leaders in their respective armies. But when Hitler and Mussolini became deranged our fathers encouraged us to seek religious careers. Same discipline, similar military order, same money. You know, there were close ties between the Axis powers and the Church. I will tell you, many of the treasures you see in this city were donated by our countries in the 1940's. Borgogno, you're Italian. You should be proud."

Borgogno and Edwards could not know that Khronin was one of the wealthiest Cardinals in Church history. His father had been a high-ranking German military official in charge of documentation and storage of looted Nazi art. He took his job seriously and protected the priceless treasures but also became rich in the process. His engineer uncles were involved in the development of

Hitler's rocket program but left with extensive documentation just before the fall of the Third Reich. They escaped any involvement in the Nuremberg trials and soon became wealthy as founders of the *Sogink Corporation*! Despite his high Church office, Hans Khronin remained a director and large shareholder of Sogink. At ordination, he had taken his priestly vows of chastity and obedience, but never a vow of poverty.

"Now I want to know…. why did you kill Francisco? How did you do it? I sent him to quiet you down, to stop the killing, and you eliminated him. By what authority did you do those things? What makes you think the world will be a better place without abortion? There are seven billion people on this planet. They will always have sex. Women will always get pregnant. There is no room on this earth for forty million more hungry mouths to feed every year. Many of those reproducing like rabbits are degenerates, scum of the earth. They would not bear the type of children who would contribute to prosperity in their nations. They are drug addicts, alcoholics and thieves. Even their own countries recognize this and fund abortions to rid themselves of this dead weight. They save maternity costs, food stamps and money for ghetto housing. I thought Francisco made those points to you in Florida. At least, he told me so after spending some days there. You seemed to understand. He told me you had promised to call off these attacks. Instead, you intensified them and killed him! Look what has happened now to the innocent children of three of the world's great statesmen. Have you no remorse?"

"Sir, The Institute for Focused Prayer was Bishop Francisco's idea. The actions flowed naturally out of that meeting" Borgogno said.

"No, it was my idea, as a PR contribution to some crazy World Prayer Month. It was not to amount to anything radical," Khronin snapped. "I have determined that neither of you can be trusted. I have no choice but to take you both out of circulation until I can decide what to do with you. Here in the Palace of the Holy Offices are a few detention cells. Most people don't know about them. They serve as temporary jails for shoplifters caught in St. Peter's Square until the Italian authorities take them to trial. I think this will be your home for a while. If I have to eliminate you, well, you can consider yourselves martys I suppose. I remind you I have complete authority over this palace. No one can overrule me but the Pope himself and he has no clue! Fortunately, it has been rumored that I may succeed him. I have befriended many of the Cardinals over the years. I think another early Pontifical retirement is fast approaching. But you, my friends, will be watching from jail. For now you'll get three meals a day and communion on Sundays." Khronin opened the large door and summoned the Swiss Guards who led the pair to adjacent holding cells in the basement. The Cardinal and his henchman left together to make their plans. Tomaso was told to have the American priests drugged one night, taken out to sea and drowned.

"Matthew," Borgogno whispered, "do you still have your phone?"

"Yes, sir. Let's see....Dammit, no bars!...Sorry, Monsignor. Forgive the cursing."

"Pass it to me. I'll raise it to the window and try. Here....one bar. Show me how to text Miguel. He's our only hope. 'Need urgent assistance. Locked up... basement of Holy Offices...JGB.' Matthew, if need be I'll offer myself as ransom and get you out of here. You need to get back to London to represent us at Windsor. Maybe my friend Miguel can get somebody to contact you with instructions on your cell phone. And now, we pray my son."

There was no return call or text and the battery was nearly dead. The men slept on their metal bunks and were awakened at dawn by the Swiss Guards with breakfast. Borgogno spoke to one of them. "Corporal, can you really follow the orders of this outlaw? Does your conscience permit this?" No reply. Then he tried in German. "We are innocent priests from America. We have committed no crimes and now we are in shoplifters' cells. Please allow us one call to the American embassy." The guards understood but did not respond. They pushed the trays into the cells and walked out.

Two armored personnel carriers rolled quietly down the back street at the Castle. In the lead vehicle was the Swiss Guard Commandant, Oberst Martin Sebastian, with a three gold star insignia on each shoulder. He was accompanied by his deputy, Major Alrig and ten soldiers. Riflemen took up positions at the Castle gate with silenced weapons. With a wave of the Commandant's hand they fired tranquilizing darts at the two traitors by the door. The lock was quickly broken and the 12 men entered the jailhouse. As they unlocked the cells, Khronin and Tomaso entered in amazement. The Cardinal began to yell at them: "Fools, you have no authority here. My word is supreme in this Castle. I answer to no one but the Pope."

Sebastian addressed him: "Your Eminence, I come at the order of the Holy Father. We are to release these prisoners and hold you both for questioning. My two treasonous guards will be court-martialed."

Tomaso drew his pistol and fired at the Commandant. Major Alrig threw himself in front of his colonel and was hit in the arm. In a split second a guard lunged at the shooter driving the long spike of his halberd through Tomaso's neck, front to back. He collapsed in a pool of blood. Several soldiers frisked the Cardinal and found a small Beretta in his waist sash. Another bandaged the arm of Major Alrig. Then Khronin was taken to a waiting armored car. Sebastian gestured, "Monsignor, allow me the privilege of escorting you and your companion to the Apostolic Palace apartment of His Holiness, Pope Roberto.

Chapter 8

Colonel Sebastian and his soldiers drove Borgogno and Edwards to the Pope's apartment. It was a bright, sunny day. They saw the large balcony overlooking St. Peter's Square where new Popes are presented to the world and give the traditional "Urbi et Orbi" sermons each Easter and Christmas. They drove through a gate protected by a large detachment of Swiss Guards and were led to a waiting elevator that took them to the Papal apartment. The apartment Guards came to strict attention as their Colonel approached then opened the door. In the greeting room stood a smiling Monsignor Miguel Jorge, the phone friend of John Borgogno and confidant of Pope Roberto, his seminary roommate. The new Pope had considered making Miguel a Cardinal but decided to keep him as his closest personal advisor.

"It's been a long time, my friend. I'm glad no harm has come to you. And you, Matthew Edwards of Pennsylvania, welcome to the Vatican. We have heard about your valiant defense of the faith and your charitable spirit. His Holiness is on the way. As you know, he chose to live in a humble guesthouse at Domus Sanctae Marthae. He shall arrive momentarily. Let's have some refreshments."

An assistant brought in iced tea and cookies and left the room. Matthew poured three teas and looked through the window curtains at the crowd gathered in St. Peter's Square. Many were taking photographs of the famous statues and iconic Papal balcony. Several white cars approached with flashing yellow lights. The crowd parted as two police cars and the Popemobile slowly approached the Apostolic Palace. People then closed in behind the procession waving and throwing flowers. The main gate was quickly locked after the entourage passed.

The heavy door opened allowing security and the Ministers of the Holy See into the room. The group split apart to make way for the Sovereign Pontiff, His Holiness, Pope Roberto. He walked in with arms outstretched and embraced his old seminary friend Miguel. "Thank you for getting us all together." Roberto used the simple "ordinary dress" for his office visits. He wore a long white cassock, a large silver cross suspended on a leather cord and a white cap. He had traded in the formal red papal shoes for his comfortable brown sandals. Instead of a gold ring on his right hand, his was a plain silver one with a cross on its face. This was a simple man of the people, humble and forgiving. He had become quickly loved at the Vatican and around the world. He had tackled the dreadful issue of priestly abuse in his first year. This Pontiff would not tolerate any misdeeds against God's children. He delivered known suspects to civilian authorities for prosecution and imprisonment and defrocked them. He was planning a worldwide prayer tour when the sensational abortion issue took center stage.

"Monsignor Borgogno and Father Edwards, I'm sorry for your recent trials and tribulations. I am ashamed that one of my Cardinals has turned against us, a modern-day Judas. And to think he was high on my succession list. A list, after one year in office! I hope I'm around a bit longer to further evaluate my closest advisors," he laughed. Matthew poured Pope Roberto an iced tea. "Gracias, Matthew" he said. Matthew's hands shook. He had never imagined meeting the Pope, now he was serving him tea in his private office. "How about a few pictures for your families? Then we'll have a conversation in the balcony room, nice chairs and a beautiful view. I want to know what you think about the recent events in Europe, Asia and America and the role of Mother Church." A secretary took several photos on an expensive digital camera. Then Matthew asked him to snap one with his cell phone. As they walked into the study Roberto waved off his staff. "No need for notes now. I just want some private conversation."

"Yes, of course, Your Holiness."

The Swiss Guards and Monsignor Jorge stayed in the outer office. The Pope closed and bolted the door to the balcony room. Borgogno and Edwards stood until he was seated and motioned for them to join him. "To the point....I want to know your positions on the mystical but violent activities going on in the world. What should I do now? The Anglicans are hosting a conference and are seen as peacemakers. I've had little to do with these events and we are called warmongers. Such things do not fit with the tenor of our last three or four Pontiffs. I am perplexed. Maybe you can give me some advice from your conclave. Now, Matthew, I read you grew up in Pennsylvania. You attended seminary in Philadelphia and were hoping for a nice assignment at a church near home. That is, until all this started?"

"Yes, Your Holiness. But I wouldn't trade my experiences this year with Monsignor and the Institute for anything. With all I've been through my faith has been strengthened and now, sir, I have met you!"

"Thank you, my son. While I speak with Monsignor you may open the doors to the balcony and take some pictures from inside. But don't go out. It will cause a commotion in the square."

"Thank you, I'd love to." Matthew slowly pulled back the doors and took out his cell phone. He tapped the camera icon. Standing back from the doorway he clicked off panoramic shots of St. Peter's Square left to right. What a sight, he thought. Then to review them he opened the phone's gallery section... three perfect shots of the crowd in the square. But the picture before those was unusual. The one snapped by the photographer in the outer office stunned him. The Pope was in the center, Matthew to the left and Monsignor to the right. The color was perfect in the whole shot except that Borgogno's face had a yellow color to it. Maybe some light from the window had caught him…… but the curtains were closed in there. He was sure of it!

"Now, Monsignor, I'd like your opinion on these serious matters. You know, I've heard of your great service and extensive travels across America. Where did you grow up?"

"Rome, sir."

"Where were you educated?"

"Rome, sir."

"Seminary?"

"Pontifical Roman opened in…."

"Yes, I know, opened in 1565 by Pope Pius IV. The school of five Popes. The Jesuit school for 'whoever desires to serve as a soldier of God.' When were you there?"

"Long ago."

"Really? But you do not wear the traditional Jesuit black robe."

"I am not a traditionalist."

"Monsignor, I'm a Jesuit. I know a Jesuit when I see one, and you're no Jesuit. Who are you?"

Incredibly, as John Gabriel Borgogo began to speak, his body turned bright yellow-white then transfigured into a glowing Angel lighting up the room. "I am a messenger, a herald." Matthew watched in amazement as the Pope prostrated himself on the carpet. Matthew knelt by the balcony door shaking. "I am Gabriel. I came from He who is and always has been. He who sent His only Son to redeem men from their sins has grown weary of the repeated wickedness. The worst offense is the slaughter of the innocents. My brother Michael has warned the world by delivering God's wrath to the continents." The intense light streaming under the Pope's locked door made the guards worry a fire had broken out. They began to bang and push on it. "Announce to all the earth abortion must stop or earthquakes and floods may end man's reign forever. Preach this message, holy Pontiff. Michael will offer a break in the destruction. Send the young one to advise world leaders. Have each nation change its ways, praise God and obey His commandments or face damnation."

The Angel took Roberto's right hand, having him stand. His other hand grasped the Pope's silver waist cross. As the Angel knelt before him, the Pope's ring and cross turned to brilliant gold. "I leave you now, holy man. Do God's will." The glowing figure turned into a blinding white orb and shot out the balcony doors into the northern sky. The Pope collapsed on the floor. The black suit and white collar of a parish priest lie folded next to him. As the Pope prayed Matthew stepped onto the balcony and saw thousands of people kneeling in St. Peter's Square singing. They had witnessed a blazing missile of hope returning to the heavens. It was now up to all nations to respond to the warning and avoid further revenge of the Angels.

CITATIONS

1. David Wallechinsky's 20th Century History With The Boring Parts Left Out. Little, Brown. ISBN 978-0-316-92056-8.
2. The Guttmacher Institute.
3. The New American Bible. Thomas Nelson, Nashville, 1969.
4. Pope Benedict XVI, address to the Pontifical Academy for Life, February 26, 2011.
5. U.S. Abortion Clock.
6. Wikipedia.

www.ingramcontent.com/pod-product-compliance
Ingram Content Group UK Ltd.
Pitfield, Milton Keynes, MK11 3LW, UK
UKHW041955230426
12048UKWH00008B/352